Flying Fish

Flying Fish

Randall Silvis

Design and Layout by Aaron Leis.
Printed and bound in England by the MPG Books Group.
Set in Adobe Caslon Pro and Greymantle

PS Publishing Ltd.
Grosvenor House
1 New Road
Hornsea, HU18 1PG
England

editor@pspublishing.co.uk
www.pspublishing.co.uk

Flying Fish

SOME RESIDENTS OF HOGG ISLAND believe that Louisa Cecelia Christensen has remained a girl well into her second century because the spider that bit her the night of her sixteenth birthday was a vampire in disguise. But Louisa Cecelia has never displayed a taste for blood, and her sauces are always prepared with an abundance of garlic, and she is frequently seen strolling hatless along the scabrous shoreline in the noontime sun.

Some say she was cursed with eternal youth by the final whimpering breath of the mother who died giving birth to her.

Some blame it on the birth caul that nearly suffocated Louisa Cecelia before her first gasp of sea air. The caul, they say, shut off all oxygen to the part of her brain that regulates growth and aging and the development of fulsome breasts, such as the ones her four sisters, all now dust, had sported so proudly and shared so freely.

In general there is no consensus among the residents of the island in regards to Louisa Cecelia's affliction, except in the generosity of their tolerance for her eccentricities and in the unspoken fear that gives birth to that generosity.

If any of the few visitors who happen onto Hogg Island during its brief and chilly summers were to come across Louisa Cecelia as she strolls the scraggly dooryards in search of bits of colored glass and other glints, or as along the shoreline she stuffs her pockets with smelly detritus, the impression left to linger would be a contradictory one. The eyes register an adolescent girl of comely face, cheeks as pink as orchard peaches, full lips poised between a smirk and a scowl, eyes as lively as a green bonfire on a moonless night. Her favorite wardrobe is an oversized L.L. Bean fisherman's vest—because of its ample pockets—over a tee-shirt of faded yellow adorned with the image of the aging pop diva Madonna, and a pair of baggy denims rolled three or four inches above the top of pink flip-flops. The aural impression, if the visitor is unlucky enough to incite a few words from Louisa Cecelia, is the sting of a tongue as sharp as that of an imperious grandmother, a vocabulary as tangy as pickle brine.

The Hoggers' secret name for Louisa Cecelia is Queenie, but it is uttered only when the doors are locked and the speaker's breath is heavy with ale, lest a night breeze blow the chide to Queenie's small but keen ears.

Louisa Cecelia is certainly old enough to be a grandmother, even a grandmother to a grandmother. But she has never married. In her long life she has been known to take only five lovers, of which only three, if the fate of the other two is any indication, gave her pleasure. She might have taken more but that she has limited herself, so far, to unmarried men between the ages of 25 and 30. Men of such age who choose to remain on the island are typically married and fathers before they graduate from high school, and the few who escape those destinies are reluctant to risk the storm of gossip that would result from fornicating with a Mesthusalehian woman who looks like a girl, a woman with an immunity to illness and death, and with, not inconsequentially, an alleged penchant for punishing lovers who fail to awaken her recalcitrant clitoris.

Take Clive McDermott and Howard Litwiler, for example. According to the bar room stories we have all heard repeated a thousand times, Litwiler, in those halcyon years before the Magnuson Act and the Fishery Management Council, was a freelance 20-something deckhand who had already established himself as a Jonah. Every captain who took him on, whether of a gillnetter, a dragger or a longliner, ended up cursing his luck. Nets snagged and ripped on reefs where no reef had ever been charted. Lines broke for no reason or became hopelessly tangled. Engines coughed and billowed black smoke. Litwiler was on the verge of souring even the most shorthanded of captains when he turned to Louisa Cecelia for a remedy. She fed him a cup of bitter tea, studied his melancholy eyes, then took him to her bed. He was not seen, nor missed, for at least a week. Then on a blustery March morning the constable received a call that some young man was out at the lighthouse, hurling stones at the high thick panes of glass. Between hurls he howled like a castrated bull. When the constable, a gentled man who had lost all three sons to the sea, climbed out of his Nash Rambler to speak with Litwiler, Howard ceased his hurling and howling, lowered his head and sprinted back toward town. The constable followed in his Rambler, only to witness Litwiler tripping over a frost heave on Main Street and diving headfirst into the town's only lamppost, there impaling his head on the broken stub of a rusty peg.

Queenie was later questioned about Litwiler's weeklong disappearance, and she readily admitted that he had spent those days in her bedroom. The constable probed for details as delicately as he could, having already surmised, appropriately or not, that Litwiler's behavior was indicative of a scorned heart. "Was there . . . intimacy?" he finally asked. Queenie fixed him, he later reported, with a look that rent his soul. He later swore that he could see the bodies of his three sons floating across the shimmer of her green eyes. "Intimacy has many forms," she told him. "Some reveal us, some redeem us, and some destroy us. Which kind interests you?" The Constable ended his questioning there and filed a report of accidental death.

Clive McDermott's death two decades earlier was not as easily explained. He had survived the carnage of Hurtgen Forest only to succumb to a tongue that, some said, wagged more effectively than his other dangling appendage. After his first night with Queenie he retreated to The Sow's Ear to regale the smoky room with wild tales of her sexual vehemence, of a carnality so aggressive that it inhibited in him the necessary tumescence. Next morning he was discovered at the base of the cliff on which our derelict lighthouse is perched. His zipper was down and his right hand still gripped, as if frozen in terror, his small and bloodless penis.

According to my father, who, when McDermott tumbled, was a young man himself, but married, the act of pissing over the cliff has always been a common moonlight indulgence for men under the influence. These days a wire cable stretches along the cliff's edge, but even so, having pressed against that strand many times in my own thirty years, sometimes sober, most times not, I can testify to the appeal of mixing urination with danger. For those few seconds, a man with a pressurized pecker in hand feels as close to godlike as he is ever to feel, and the arc he sends off the precipice engenders both divine relief and a brief illusion of potency in an otherwise impotent life.

That the crabs had not by morning completely nibbled off McDermott's penis suggested that he had fallen no more than an hour or so prior to his discovery. Three fingernails from his left hand had been torn out, and later that day his brother was lowered on a rope to look for those nails in the tender bark of the roots protruding from the cliff face. Only one fingernail was recovered but it was sufficient to suggest that McDermott had indeed clung to that particular root before either gravity or despair finally seduced him lower. The mystery of whether he had lacked the presence of mind to let go of his pecker and seize the root with both hands, or had grabbed his pecker for comfort, as men are prone to do, just an instant before impact, has never been solved.

As to the specifics of the tales reputedly told at The Sow's Ear by the fallen man the night before his death, only unappetizing morsels remain, and these I will not repeat, for even though I, like most residents of Hogg Island, have freely engaged in the pastime of outlandish gossip, speculation and unabashed fabrication in regards to Louisa Cecelia's sexual practices, I do so no longer. Moreover I have come to doubt that the freakish deaths of those former Hoggers were in any way related to their unsuccessful liaisons with her.

On the other hand, maybe she, like most who survive the buffeting and erosion of too many years, has acquired a more compassionate view than the one practiced when she was younger. It may be that she has repudiated revenge and now punishes by subtler means those who dissatisfy her. I can only hope that this is the case.

The wind was high and the sky blue-black and the boats were all lashed in their slips on the day my brother made the suggestion that would change my life. "Just look at Manfred Rudy," Jasper said. "What do you think he's doing now?"

"I know what he's doing as well as you do."

We were sitting across from each other in a booth at The Sow's Ear, ten or so in the morning. Because of the salt film frosting the outside of the windows and the smoke film blurring the inside, it seemed like half-past midnight. The air was thick with the exhaust from cigarettes and the grease from the deep fryers that were turning out one basket of smelts and chips after another for the two dozen restless men consigned to shore for the day.

"He's pulling down 40K a year is what he's doing."

"In New Bed," I said.

"Yeah in New Bed. What the fuck is wrong with New Bedford?"

I sipped my beer. It tasted flat. "He works on a garbage truck. What's so great about that?"

"Six hour days, that's what's so great about it. Start at five, done before noon. Forty fucking K a year. When was the last time you saw forty fucking K?"

I sipped my beer. "A guy could get lung cancer in this place."

"How about Crowley?" he said.

"Crowley's got a bum leg, remember?"

"It's a bum hip actually. Came down hard off the last step at St. Peter's."

"I was fucking there, Jasper. Same as you."

"So he goes to the emergency room and then what?"

"Not much apparently. He's still got a bad hip."

"And what else does he have?"

I pushed my beer away. It was turning bitterer with every sip. "Fuck Crowley," I said.

"That's my point exactly. Queenie fucked Crowley, Crowley jams his hip, Crowley goes to the emergency room and meets the new nurse. The nurse falls in love with him, they get married, and now Crowley's down in Amherst going to college on a big fat scholarship her daddy arranged for him."

"You don't know for certain that those guys shagged Queenie."

"Everybody knows."

"Nobody knows for certain. Just like nobody knows for certain about Schmelz back in the seventies. Or about McDermott and Litwiler before him."

"We know that McDermott and Litwiler died ugly," he said. "And that Schmelz made a fortune on the internet bubble."

"But nobody knows for certain that any of it was because of Queenie."

"You want to know what's for certain? Poverty is for certain, asshole. Misery is for certain. One of us, maybe both of us are going to die out there on *The Egg* someday if we keep doing what we're doing. That's about as certain as certain gets."

"You want Queenie shagged? So do it yourself."

"I've got a wife. With a belly about to pop for the third fucking time. Besides . . . ."

"Besides what?"

7

"Let me ask you something," he said. "You actually prefer this miserable dead-end existence?"

"Beats the alternative."

"It beats one alternative."

"There are others?"

"Get off this fucking turd of an island. That's the best alternative."

"Get off with what? My charm and good looks?"

At last glance there were one hundred and twelve dollars in my checking account. Zero dollars in the savings account. No 401K, no IRA, no stocks or bonds, no stash of Krugerrands, no golden parachute, not a pot to piss in, as our father used to say. Jasper paid for my medical insurance but his wife Belinda had made it clear to both of us that once the new baby arrived, I would be, as she put it, booted off the gravy train.

"Your charm and good looks might be more valuable than you think," he said. "Not that I find you the least bit attractive."

"Fuck you," I told him.

"I have a better idea. Fuck Queenie."

I flashed him my most disgusted look but it had no effect. He wasn't smiling, wasn't scowling, just sat there staring at me like he could see through walls. Like he could see the rooms full of misery inside my heart. So I studied the tabletop instead. It was scarred and greasy, fork-gouged and knife-carved. I had been coming here and sitting in this booth since before I could walk. Sat on a red plastic booster seat while our dad got drunk and our mother got drunker. Now both of them were gone, Mom in the cemetery and Dad reduced to fish shit on the ocean floor. And here Jasper and I still sat. He and Belinda lived in our old house on Leviathan Road. I lived above The Sow's Ear in a room that stank of fried smelts and cancer sticks.

Jasper leaned toward me over the table. "And don't you sit there and try to fucking tell me that you have higher standards than that."

"I never said a word."

He seemed angry all of a sudden. "Because I have been with you on the Cape," he said. "I've seen the skanks you let drag you home at night."

"They're college girls, for Christ's sake."

"Right. Skanky degenerate college girls. They have to get shitfaced before they can let themselves enjoy a man with a hard body for a change. That's the only way they can forgive themselves for sinking so low. And you. Jesus."

"What about me?"

"You think you're actually stepping up in life when you fuck one of them. That's the fucking pity of it."

What I wanted to say right then was, And just what do you know of loneliness, brother? What do you understand about the hunger and hollowness and longing for human touch? But what I said instead was, "So I'm supposed to be too good for them? Is that what you're saying?"

"Fuck no. That's my point exactly."

"You have a point? Because you're not making any sense at all as far as I can tell."

"My point, little brother, is that I'm no prize and neither are you. We keep drinking a gallon of beer a day and we're both going to end up looking like Dad. Fuck, I'm already halfway there and you're not far behind. We keep inhaling these fumes and we're going to end up on either side of Mom."

"Mom smoked two packs a day."

"And how much of what she smoked have we both already inhaled? And how much more in this fucking place? And you live upstairs, for fuck's sake!"

"If you're so unhappy here, Jasper, why don't *you* just pick up and leave?"

He leaned back against the plywood wall. He looked me dead in the eye. "We're going to," he said.

I wasn't sure I had heard him right. Somebody had slipped a coin into the jukebox and Eric Clapton was bitching his heart out to George Harrison's wife. "You're going to what?"

"Rudy's wife told Belinda she can get her a job as a receptionist with that accountant she works for. After the baby, I mean. Six or seven months from now."

"And what are you going to do? Stay home and babysit?"

"They've got daycare over there. Good schools. Restaurants. Air that doesn't stick in your throat and clog up your lungs."

"You still haven't told me what you plan to do."

He just looked at me. There was something like a smile on his lips, but the thing that would have made it a smile was missing. Suddenly I realized why.

"You're not," I said. "You're fucking not."

"His company put a bid out for two more routes. Rudy says it's a lock. In which case they'll be looking for another man."

"You're going to pick up other people's garbage for a living?"

"Forty fucking K a year."

"Shit-filled diapers and spoiled food and holey underwear and tissues full of snot and—"

"What do I do now?" he asked. His face was tight and he was leaning toward me again. His voice was as pained as Clapton's but there was no music in it.

"What do I handle now, man? What do you handle now? Slimy fish skin, stinking fish guts, putrid bait, crap we haul in and can't even identify? You think that's any better? I can't fucking stand it anymore. It turns my stomach every time I have to walk down to that fucking dock."

"So go live in New Bed and pick up garbage. Sell me *The Egg*."

The boat's full name was *Mona's Nest Egg*, and for a while maybe, one or two good seasons when we were kids, it had promised to be just that. But I was fourteen when Mom got sick, seventeen when Dad got careless, and ever since then the family's luck has been going from pathetic to fucking pathetic.

"*The Egg*'s upside down, asshole. I owe more on it than it's worth."

"We paid that boat off with Dad's insurance money."

"Yeah and what paid for the new engine three years ago? What pays to fix the equipment every time something breaks or tears? What pays to put fuel in the tank every time the price goes up fifty cents a gallon? You think the few fucking fish we catch pays to feed my family?"

"Have you been borrowing money to pay me, Jasper?"

He looked away for a moment. "The fucking deck boards are rotten, Devon. Every piece of equipment we have is obsolete. Slip rental alone costs almost a dollar a day. The government keeps shortening our season and closing off our fishing grounds. Georges Bank, Nantucket Shoals, the Eastern End—who knows what's next? They're not going to stop until the only place us draggermen can drop our nets is in our own fucking bathtubs. And you know what, brother?"

He blew out a breath. It looked smoky to me.

"As far as I'm concerned, it can't happen soon enough."

I sat there a while, too numb for a complete thought. Finally I reached for his empty bottle and gathered it up with mine and the other four empties. As I carried them toward the bar he said, "I don't want any more beer."

A couple of minutes later I set a cup of coffee in front of him, then eased back down with my own cup. After a while he said, "I'm sorry. I'm sorry but I had to tell you sooner or later." He turned his coffee cup in one full circle. "Maybe I'm just getting old, I don't know."

I kept sliding my feet across the floor, just to make sure it was still there. "You're only thirty-three."

If he had any answer to that I didn't hear it. I was staring at the eye looking back at me from my coffee, and "Free Bird" was blaring out of the jukebox. If there had been more than four dollars in my pocket I would have handed it to the bartender then kicked the shit out of the juke. When the music finally stopped I could swear I heard a dull kind of sucking sound inside my head. I longed for my narrow bed upstairs. I longed for a dark room that would close me in and stop up my senses.

"Besides," Jasper said. "Your heart was never really into this work anyway."

I wanted to look up at him but my head felt too heavy, my neck too weak to lift it.

"I mean what about all those poems you write when we're out on the water? Maybe you could get them published or something."

I let my eyes close. Maybe I could go to sleep right there. Maybe if I breathed in enough cigarette smoke it would put me down forever.

"But hell," he said. "Truth is I never understood those poems. Besides, you said it yourself a hundred times, right? Nobody reads poetry, so what fucking good is it? What you need to do is to write a novel. Isn't that what you always said you really want to do? Write your *Moby Dick?*"

I laughed a sour laugh. There was no *Moby Dick* in me and I knew it. Not even a Charlie Tuna. Out on *The Egg* I had occasionally tossed off a couple lines of mediocre free verse, and yes, had fantasized aloud about joining the ranks of those authors whose books line the walls of my little room, but the few times I had actually sat down with a notebook on my lap and a pen in hand, my brain produced nothing but a slow leak of air, and before long the sucking sound would begin in my head, and my noble intentions would deteriorate into doodles of waterspouts, mermaids and fish with jagged wings.

"All you really need," Jasper said, which made me believe that he too could see the vast emptiness in my brain, "is something to write about. Something *worth* writing about. You ever think of that?"

He was silent so long, sitting there waiting, that I finally opened my eyes, cranked my head up, and lifted my smoky gaze to his.

"Me," he said, "I can think of only one thing around here that's worth writing about. But it *is* damn interesting, you have to admit. She's the most interesting damn thing I've ever heard of."

This much was true. Even though we had grown up with Queenie in our midst we never tired of talking about her, never wearied of wondering about the nature of her affliction. Was it demonic or divine? Chemical or electrical? I had read quite a few pages about progeria, the disease that ages people prematurely, makes a nine-year-old appear a frail and withered ninety. But numerous midnight hours of surfing the internet had never revealed the existence of its antithesis, not a single documented case of progeria turned inside out.

Louisa Cecelia had never been documented because we Hoggers kept her condition secret. We protected it, hoarded it, shared it with each other but concealed it from the world. Our mothers and fathers had taught us to do so, just as theirs had taught them. Why? Because, whether with good reason or not, they had feared her. And because they had, we did. But she was also cherished. We were not merely a hardscrabble village on Hogg Island, we were a world apart, a universe unto ourselves. We mistrusted outsiders. Most of us were related, second and third and fourth cousins to one another. The Christensens were bound by blood to the Leavitts, the Leavitts to the Hawkins, the Hawkins to the McDermotts . . . . Queenie was ours and we were hers. She read our fortunes, mixed poultices and other herbal remedies. She warned men when to stay off the water on a stone-calm day. When Jasper's wife wanted to know the gender of the baby she was carrying, she didn't take a boat to the mainland and get an ultrasound, she walked downstreet and pressed a fiver into Queenie's little hand.

In this way, I guess, we all felt a part of Queenie's longevity. She was the thread that ran through the generations. She was our little girl, our impossibly ancient crone. She made us special.

And now here was my brother advising me to exploit her oddity for personal gain. Strangely, ashamedly, I found the notion intriguing. "Yes but what do you think Queenie would do if she found out I was writing about her?"

Jasper grinned. "Aren't writers supposed to take risks? Sacrifice comfort for risk or something like that?"

"I don't have any comfort to sacrifice."

"Then you've got nothing to lose, do you?"

"No more, I suppose, than Litwiler and McDermott lost."

"So now you believe those stories? Now when it suits your argument?"

I shrugged. "It's a moot point anyway. Takes two to tango, you know."

His grin widened. "Last time Belinda went to see her?"

I looked at him.

"She said, So what's going on with Devon these days? He involved with anyone?"

"Belinda said that?"

"Queenie said that."

"Like hell she did."

"Ask Belinda."

"Sure, because the two of you cooked this up."

"I swear to God we didn't. I mean think about it. Crowley was the last one as far as we know. And that's been what—two years now?"

"The last one as far as we know. It's not like she announces it in the *Gazette*."

"Don't we always know though? Everybody always knows. She's never tried to hide her affairs. Just like she didn't try hiding her interest in you."

"So why me?"

"I don't know why you. Because she's scraping the bottom of the barrel, how the fuck would I know?"

"Seems to me you're claiming to know."

"Listen, do the math. Three hundred eighty-seven people on the whole fucking island. Let's say half of them male. Of the ones over eighteen, most of us are married. She's never picked a married man, a man in a serious relationship, or a man over thirty. So who does that leave?"

"There's Pudge Wilkinson."

"So there's you and a twenty-four-year old stockboy who can't tell the difference between a can of dog food and a can of clam chowder. Who would you pick?"

"You sure know how to instill confidence in a man, Jasper."

Truth was, I didn't need Jasper's help to lower my confidence. All my life I had been looking at the world, and myself, through a pair of eyes turned toward my nose. It was a mild case of strabismus that caused me no real visual impairment other than occasional double vision and a tendency to squint in dim settings. The squinting, or so I had been told in the

13

dusklight of various mainland barrooms, gave me a brooding, troubled, James Dean-like look that various drunken college girls found appealing. In the light of morning, though, when I regarded myself in the mirror, I failed to see the charm of it.

Jasper said, "Maybe what really worries you is your ability to get the job done. You don't have one of those micro-peters, do you?"

"You tell me. You've seen me piss in the ocean at least five times a week."

"I'd say you've got the equipment if you know how to use it. So what are you worried about?"

"How about getting a lamppost stuck to my forehead?"

"No worries there," Jasper said. "Queenie's never killed the same way twice."

The conversation with my brother took place on a Friday morning. In mid-afternoon I dragged myself out of The Sow's Ear and trudged toward my pickup truck in the corner of the lot, meaning to take a drive around the island just to clear my head. But instead of climbing in behind the wheel I stood there atop the crushed shells, remained a few feet from my truck as if held in place by an invisible force field. I had bought my 12-year-old quarter-ton Ford third hand five years earlier, when its surface was already pitted and rusted, the faded blue paint already chipped and scratched and dented. The driver's side mirror was broken off, both taillights burned out. The engine burned oil and churned black smoke out the tailpipe, the floorboards had a gaping hole rusted through, and the muffler scraped the pavement whenever I carried a passenger. And I was still making payments on it.

The thought dawned on me then—though the phrase *dawned on me* hardly captures the wash of nausea that churned through my stomach—that if I climbed into that truck one more time I would never climb out of the life it had come to epitomize. The truck was the emblem of my dystymia, a sucking black hole whose event horizon lay just two paces forward.

I backed away from it. And I kept walking backward until my feet hit the macadam of the shore road. Then I made a half turn and walked forward. I walked with the gray wind at my back for a while, until, after rounding the northeast end of the island, I walked with the wind in my face. I walked past squat weathered houses, past scraggly yards where stunted oaks leaned seaward, looking for all the world like old men who longed to fling themselves into the deep. I walked past windblown garbage, plastic bags stuck to bushes, empty beer and soft drink cans, somebody's old tennis shoe. I walked past three crows squabbling over what might have been a flattened squirrel. Past the abandoned lighthouse with every pane of glass smashed out long ago, the front door torn off its hinges and rotting in the high grass. Without even looking I could envision the filthy interior of that tower, just as every under-aged drinker on the island could, every sex-crazed couple without a backseat or bed.

I was surprised to notice so many houses with their windows boarded shut. The erosion of the island's population was something we were all aware of in a peripheral kind of way, but the cumulative effect of all those lifeless homes drove a chill of despair deep into my bones.

I walked past the two-room school where I had been taught nothing useful. The overlook where, at sixteen, on an army surplus blanket in the predawn mist, I had lost my virginity to an overweight girl named Marsha. She cried afterward and told me she loved me. When I failed to respond in kind, she called me a skinny little cross-eyed faggot. Maybe she was why I preferred drunken college girls; I never had to face them at school the next day.

I walked and I walked. By twilight I had completed a full circuit of the island, just over three and a half miles with frequent layovers to gaze at the rocks and the sea, at the low-hanging adumbration of sky.

I do not know the time nor recall the urge that incited me to turn off the shore road and trudge inland. Maybe there was no thought at all, just a heavy hollowness that canted me sidewards. I do know that I felt like weeping, felt like dropping to my knees and lapsing into sweet unconsciousness. But I knew no chants for self-annihilation. I carried no poisons, no firearms. Not even a penknife for sawing away at my arteries. In lieu of those escapes, I knocked on Queenie's door.

As a child I had walked past her small house countless times. Had stared at it, scrutinized it, watched her coming and going as all Hoggers do. We imagined that the grass grew somehow thicker in her yard than in our own, was a more vibrant shade of green. Certainly her flowerbed and tiny garden plot were more orderly and productive than most, her picket fence and all that it enclosed much neater.

There were no mounds of dog shit in Queenie's yard, no feral cats cowering under the porch. From the road her home looked like an oversized dollhouse, built for her by her father the year before he died, erected atop the filled in foundation of the Christensen family home that had burned to the ground, taking both of her brothers with it.

The story of that incident ran through my head as I waited at her door. Queenie and her father—he well into his sixties by then, she nearing forty—had gone to the mainland to see the candlelit Christmas illuminations. All that is known about the conflagration that consumed the Christensen home is this: Two hours before the flames lit up the island, her brothers, already roaring drunk, were seen leaving The Sow's Ear with four quarts of beer in hand. What was left of the brothers in the morning was plowed into the stone foundation along with the rest of the clapboard house, then covered over with rocky soil. The site was left to settle for a year, during which time Queenie and her father lived with one of the married sisters. Finally her father built the dollhouse single-handedly, planing every board and pounding every nail, setting the cupboards low enough for a child to reach the highest shelf, fashioning furniture that was a perfect fit for Queenie's diminutive frame.

Until that night when a despairing circumambulation of the island brought me to her door, I had seen only the exterior of the house. Many people though had stepped into the front room, where Queenie gave her readings and dispensed her herbal remedies. But none ever described it as anything but unexceptional, a typical parlor other than its low ceiling and small furniture. Of the five men who allegedly shared her bed for a time, three refused to utter a word about the experience. The other two were worm shit.

It was an utter indifference to the latter fate, maybe even an attraction to it, that raised my knuckles to her door that night.

The door squeaked open by no more than two inches, just enough for the left side of Queenie's face to appear. Her mouth might have been smiling; even now I can't be sure.

"I was wondering if I could get a reading," I said. "I'm sorry if it's late, I . . . I've been out walking for a while."

"Is it late?" she asked.

"I, uh . . . . I don't really know. It feels late, I guess." Like most Hoggers I wear no wristwatch. We timed our lives by the sun and the tides.

"It feels late for what?" she asked.

I could think of no reply. There was something disconcerting about the way she looked up at me, the way she spoke. Her voice was softer and far less caustic than I had expected, in fact as mellifluous as a girl's, and her face, still as pink and unwrinkled as a teenager's, certainly matched the voice, but the left eye held me in its gaze and made me feel small, somehow reversed the visible fact that she was the shorter one. She stood no higher than my chin yet seemed to loom over me. I wanted to cow and back away. Yet felt a simultaneous urge to fall into and be engulfed by her.

She looked at me a few moments longer. Then turned away and disappeared. But left the door standing open.

Half a minute later I laid my hand on the door's edge and gave a timid push. The door swung wide. Queenie was now sitting at a small oak table near the center of a room of maybe one hundred square feet. The only other furniture was a bentwood rocker beside a gas heater, and in front of the window a small sofa, a green brocaded love seat. Cream-colored curtains framed the windows. A braided oval rug covered most of the plank floor.

Only two chairs accompanied the table. The chair to Queenie's right was a different size than hers, was built low to the ground like hers but with a seat large enough to accommodate an adult of normal size. The room felt warm and snug. A small floor lamp in the southern corner gave the room its only light.

From just inside her door I could now see into the kitchen, the low cabinets and sink, the two-burner stove, the wide, squat refrigerator. None of this surprised me. What made the breath snag in my chest was the sight of Queenie herself.

She was wearing a pink terrycloth robe with matching bedroom slippers. Her hair, which I had hitherto seen only piled into an unruly chestnut bundle, with loose strands writhing in a tangled argument with the wind that always seems to blow here, now hung freely about her shoulders. The soft light picked up the traces of auburn and made them shine. And her face . . . . No scowling mouth, no squinting suspicious eyes, no imperious lift to the finely sculptured chin. She appeared nothing less than a very pretty girl fresh from the bath. I stepped inside—anyway I assume that I did; I must have, though nothing that happened from this point on remains a clear and trusted memory—and closed the door. A vague scent of strawberries reached my nose. Something deep inside me groaned.

"You're hungry," she said.

"No, I . . . . I don't think so."

"You're hungry, Devon." But she offered me nothing to eat. "Come sit."

I crossed to her and lowered myself onto the empty chair.

"Give me your hand."

"Right or left?"

"You think they tell different stories?"

She wrapped both of her small hands around mine. The warmth caught me by surprise, the cleanliness, the softness. A whimper emerged through my lips.

Her mouth turned up at the corners. "How much do you want to know?"

"How much? Well . . . everything, I guess."

"Everything is too much."

"Too much . . . money? Or too much for me to handle or . . . . I'm not sure I understand."

"If you understood you wouldn't be here now."

Her words were making me dizzy. I laughed uncomfortably. "I want to know about my life, I guess. What I'm supposed to do with it."

"You're supposed to live it," she said.

"Yes but . . . ." She had not released my hand. Had not broken eye contact. I felt tiny beside her, a fledgling in her hand.

"Aren't you living your life?" she asked.

"I don't know. I guess I'm not."

"How do you know you're not?"

"That's just it, I don't know. I don't seem to know anything at all."

"Do you know why you came here?"

"Well . . . to get a reading, I guess."

She smiled again. Her hands kept mine enclosed but remained perfectly still. "I know you, Devon," she said.

I couldn't help myself, I winced and looked away. The urge to weep was growing stronger, filled my head with congestion, made my chest ache, my eyes sting. Just when I thought I could hold it back no longer and was going to start sobbing, she released my hand. My head cleared in an instant, so quickly that I jerked upright as if jolted awake. I looked at her but it seemed as if my eyes were more crossed than usual.

"Some people live in their bodies," she said. "Some in their hearts. You live in your head."

I blinked several times to bring the room back into focus. "Is that a bad thing?"

She continued to smile at me. By degrees my vision cleared. In fact it achieved a clarity unlike any I had experienced. All my senses seemed suddenly tuned to a higher frequency, so that every detail of texture and line, every scrape of wind outside her house, every breath of strawberry scent seemed experienced in every cell of my body.

She asked, "Are you willing to admit yet why you came here tonight?"

"I . . . I want to but . . . ."

She took hold of my left hand then. She slid her chair back and stood and came close to me. With her right hand she undid the cloth belt and let her robe fall open. Her breasts were small but perfect in their smallness, her stomach flat. A scattering of fine curly hairs formed an inverted triangle below a perfect navel. Her skin was as smooth as polished marble, except that marble is cold and the warmth that emanated from Louisa Cecelia was tropical.

She moved so close that her breast brushed my cheek. The nipple felt as sharp as an icicle, as hot as a blade. "Do you know why you came?" she asked.

I felt myself swooning but I managed two words. "I do."

Her bedroom was in every way the antithesis of the parlor. Atop a small cherrywood dresser burned three squat candles evenly spaced apart. Here the scent of strawberries was redolent, released from the melting wax to be carried high on the heat from the sputtering flames. The bed took up most of the floor space, a wide bed maybe twelve inches longer than Queenie was tall. The bed was neatly made but with the quilted coverlet turned back—by all appearances a bedroom made ready for assignation. Had she somehow known I would come here tonight? Had she somehow summoned me?

And as if I was not already dizzy enough, the walls alone would have undone me. The parlor walls were virtually bare, an earth-toned paint above knotty pine wainscoting. But on every wall here, arranged in no apparent pattern, no geometry of order yet somehow placed as to give an impression of indecipherable harmony, were shadowboxes of every size from matchbox to windowpane, shoe box size and playing card size and egg carton size and book size and every size in between, all hung on the walls from ceiling to within a couple feet of the floor. Hundreds of them in total. The contents of each box were illuminated by a flickering candle of appropriate size, some candles placed atop the shadowboxes, some on bottom ledges, some in corners, but all so placed that the lights too, when viewed as a whole from the doorway—where I was more than momentarily stunned into a blinking pause—seemed a precisely disordered pattern of lights, as soothing to the eye as a clear night sky over water, but a sky creased and shaped into a box itself, this shadowbox of a room.

Only when I studied the shadowboxes individually was the harmony warped by dissonance. One box held a broken ceramic mantel clock with only the minute hand intact, a porcelain baby doll's head turned to consider the clock, the hair sprayed out and stiffened in a parody of fright, a lobster's fighting claw dangling from a piece of fishing line as if sneaking up from behind to pinion the baby doll's severed neck, and, most incongruous of all, a naked Barbie doll's headless body lying supine with a long shard of green beer bottle glass protruding from her nonexistent vagina.

In another box, a collage of tiny photos, headshots cropped from magazines and glued together in five concentric circles, a hundred or more smiling countenances of celebrities and politicos, each photo placed so that its subject was smiling at the photo to its right, a pinwheel of artificial smiles that went round and round like a labyrinth to culminate at its center in a single bloodshot eyeball staring back at the viewer.

My gaze moved from box to box, from displays containing bits of rock or shell, broken cups and dishes, words and phrases clipped from newspapers, shreds of clothing, cracked cd jewel cases, empty medicine bottles, dried flowers, fish skeletons, starfish, pieces of jewelry, tarnished flatware, unidentifiable things. All in all, a kaleidoscopic display of shadowbox art, but too much at once; brain-addling.

I looked away, blinked and blinked. I tried to focus on the window. Looked back at a wall. Felt myself falling into this sputtering flame or that, into this or that shadowbox. The colors, the candles, the strawberry air . . . .

Louisa Cecelia lay waiting on her bed. Her smile drew me nearer. Each hesitant step seemed a lurch that might pull me off my feet. She lay there in the center of the wide bed, the pink robe fully open now, the cloth spread out beneath her like folded pink wings. Her small body seemed framed by the mattress, a tiny perfect figure in a shadowbox of padded white, legs crossed at the ankles, wrists crossed, hands cupping her breasts. I heard a thundering of crashing waves inside my head, felt a buffeting of wind. The wind shoved me toward her, pushed me back. I swayed for and aft. Am I drunk? I asked myself. What day is this?

She seemed so small lying there, so young.

"I am not a child," she said.

Had I spoken aloud? "I know. It's just . . . ."

She raised her right foot toward me. I reached for it, grasped the delicate ankle, held on for dear life. She bent her knee toward her chest then and drew me onto the bed, pulled me atop her. The candles sputtered and cracked. I tasted strawberries. Her little hands flew over me like ravenous bats.

How long we continued, I cannot say. No time existed in that room, only movement and touch, sensation and gasp. Surely hours passed. Enough time at least that I surprised myself with my stamina and self-control. My body grew slick with perspiration but did not tire. My sweat dripped onto her stomach, glazed her skin. We moved with ease from one position to the next, with her on her back, then stomach, then knees, then atop me facing the window, facing the door. I could feel the momentum slowly building inside her, the urgency like a low wave moving out from the African coast, picking up water, picking up heat, tumbling over and over itself as it rolled past Europe, growing as it swept past South America, swelling as it flooded the Caribbean.

When the wave of pleasure crashed ashore on the Atlantic coast it was a hundred feet high. I was standing beside the bed then, her hips elevated by two pillows, her ankles resting on my shoulders. I felt the wave taking hold of me, driving us together, throwing both of us into the airless clouds to hold our breath and plummet, plummet, spinning and tumbling through our high white death.

In the afterward, the slow falling away, she stared at me open-eyed. Her stomach muscles quivered, her thigh muscles twitched. And for a few timeless moments her eyes took on a brilliant clarity. I saw in them then an intelligence as clear and potent as hundred proof gin. But soon her body quieted, relaxed, and she let it sink onto the bed. I slipped out of her. Moaned. Felt lost. Unsteady on my feet.

She closed her eyes.

I stood there a while trying to recover my breath, my balance. But my legs felt watery, not made for standing, and I eased myself down. When she opened her eyes and looked at me again her eyes were different. As clear as gin in a frosted glass. I do not mean to imply by this that her eyes became cloudy, they did not. But the intelligence they had revealed just minutes earlier now seemed reclaimed, withdrawn out of reach of any man's gaze.

❧

I lay beside her with only our fingertips touching. I lay there looking at the moon high on her window. It was white and cool and I wanted to salve my blistered tongue against it. I thought about standing up to do so but I could not. Men stand and I was not a man. Then what was I? I saw myself as a dog of some kind, feral, bloody muzzled. The scent of her bed was keen in my nose, damp soil, ocean breeze, and the sounds of her little house tumbled against each other in my ears, the creak of dry boards, the plink of her tin roof shrinking ever so slightly as it gave up its heat to the cool of night. I tasted warm melon in my mouth, the pale white rind of her lips, the pale orange meat of her tongue. At that moment I was only what I saw and smelled and heard and tasted. I am the tree frog chirping from the yard next door. I am the fat white moth hurling itself against the window in the front room where the bulb of the floor lamp burns like a dry expiring sun. But I was aware of my brain too, a consciousness of self that seemed to have shrunk into a wavering shadow, for there was no chattering of man thoughts, only images of awareness sparked by my senses—the little green frog in a fork of slender branches some six feet off the ground, the white smudge of moth dust on the windowpane.

Then for a moment this hollow space of my mind was filled by a sound. *Come back tomorrow.* I rolled my head to the side and looked at her. She appeared to be asleep, was breathing with the slow regularity of an innocent child. Had she spoken? A tenderness for her swept through me, it stripped me raw. But on its heels came a revulsion for what I had done. An instant later a sickening fear as I wondered if she was a demon in disguise, a Hogg Island succubus who turns men into whimpering dogs and devours their souls.

The longer I watched her, the more I became a man again. The more I grew ashamed of my nakedness. I was ashamed too of the certainty that

I would accede to her wishes. I thought to ask, *What time tomorrow?* but knew in an instant the answer, the same time, it will always be the same time now. Until she grew tired of me or I displeased her it would always be the same time.

I dressed quietly beside the bed and I vacated the house quietly. I walked maybe five hundred yards through the dark before I let myself down in the corner of the yard of a man I knew. I could hear the man's wife snoring in her bedroom in the back of the house. I could hear the man snoring from the couch in the living room. The moon was well out of reach for both man and canine now but my tongue no longer felt blistered and the taste of melon was metallic now. I laid my face to the ground and opened my mouth to the grass. I breathed in its moisture and scent, its salty taste. I was heavy with sadness and heavy with the beauty of a black sky pricked by stars. I wanted to weep but I was too sad for tears. The air smelled of foaming waves that died crashing on the rocks. Every thunderous beat hammered my skin.

In the gray light of morning I made my way to the dock. I stood on the edge of the *The Egg*'s slip, staring down at sloshing water, benumbed. Time passed. "Morning, brudda," Jasper said. I could barely find the strength, or the memory of how the mechanism worked, to turn his way.

"Christ, you look like shit," he said.

I wanted to speak, mutter a confession, but all I could accomplish was to run my tongue over parchment lips.

A look of alarm came into his eyes. He held up a hand. "Don't say a word. Not one fucking word. You know what happens to the men who talk about her afterward."

I blinked helplessly.

He came closer and kept his voice low. "You did it, didn't you? Wait, don't tell me, don't even fucking nod. I know you did it. Fuck, I never thought you would. Shit, man. I mean holy fucking mother of fuck. What happens now?"

I asked the same question but only with my eyes.

"Go home," he said. "Really, Devon, go back to your place and sleep or something. You'd be a menace to me and yourself today."

He patted my bristled cheek. "I never thought you'd fucking do it," he said. He turned away, crossed to the aft cleat, undid the line, seemed in a hurry to separate himself from me. "I'll say a prayer to Poseidon for you, okay?"

He came back to the forward cleat, then cast a glance at the blue sky yawning open through a rising mist. "Now please move away before we both get struck by lightning."

My room seemed half its usual size, the threadbare sofa and thrift store table, the hot plate and enameled sink, the narrow mattress on its metal frame. The walls, I noticed, were marbled with adumbrations, the stains from ten thousand nights of barroom smoke, irregular suggestions of gray that now seemed like shadows struggling to push themselves out through the wallboard and paint. I had an urge to trace those shadows with a felt-tip pen, outline the spirits emanating, a long-necked wolf, a human face with a pair of lopsided eyes, a severed foot, a fallen tree . . . .

But I was too exhausted to look for a pen. Instead I lay on my mattress and outlined the shadows with my gaze. When it became a struggle to keep my eyes open I took a last glance at the clock beside the bed. Seven-forty-two a.m. And I closed my eyes.

I awoke at exactly 2:47 in the afternoon. I should have felt rested but I did not, for I had dreamed that I was awake and trying unsuccessfully to sleep. But a story had formed in my head. I could see clearly the first scene of the story and knew somehow that the rest of it was waiting behind that scene, eager to be revealed.

I made a cup of instant coffee, found a tablet and pen, sat down at the table. Three hours passed. What was in my head seemed to flow down my neck, through my arm and hand and the pen and onto the paper. It started as images but came out as words. When the words stopped coming I saw that I had a story, my first complete story, a weird little tale that felt both mine and wholly alien to me. I was left with a feeling at once pleasurable and sad. A familiar feeling, though, for I had always felt the same way afterward with the girls from the Cape. I wanted to get inside and stay inside each one as deeply as possible, squeeze two lonely souls together into a single smiling one. But as the smile quickly faded, and it always did, we would look at each other and think, I have no idea who you are.

It was the same with the story. I read it over a couple of times, changed words and phrases, excised lines that made me wince. By the time I finished I was excited again, even more exhausted but mildly aroused, and thinking of Louisa Cecelia.

"It's called 'When Love Is Blind.'"

"Go ahead," she said.

She was lying naked on the bed, propped on a hip and elbow. I was still fully dressed, rolled sheaf of papers in hand, standing next to the chair by the window in her candlelit room.

"You want me to read it to you?"

"Please."

"You wouldn't rather read it yourself?"

She rolled onto her back, closed her eyes, crossed her hands over her breasts. "Seduce me," she said.

I set a candle on the windowsill, sat and leaned into the light. Here is what I read:

> When I awoke in the middle of the night to find someone in bed beside me, I thought at first that she must be my wife. I am not the kind of man who invites other women into his marriage bed. But I had spoken with my wife on the telephone just two hours earlier; she was in another city, six hundred miles away—her first day of a week-long business trip to select the autumn inventory for a local boutique. She had said then that she was going to call room service for a sandwich and a glass of Bordeaux, do a bit of reading, and go to bed.
>
> Then who was this woman beside me? Even in the absolute darkness of my bedroom there was no question as to gender: her warmth, the smooth rub of her thigh against mine, the vague scent of roses I inhaled with every breath. I did not immediately turn to look at her but lay there frozen on my back, balanced, I felt, on the icy blade of my spine, asking myself if I was truly awake or only dreaming I had awakened. There was none of the typical disorientation one experiences when

on the threshold of sleep; the room did not appear canted or the door in the wrong place; everything was as it should have been except that there was a strange woman sharing my bed, lying not on my right, where my wife always slept, but on the opposite side.

Was she, I wondered, some new kind of burglar? A kissing bandit who goes all the way? The apartment door was triple-locked, all windows bolted; we were on the seventh floor of a security building. There was no way in or out that did not require my complicity.

I have to admit that my first reaction was one of fear. But the scent that rose on its own warmth from beneath the covers, the warmth that radiated from her body, invading my pores, heating my flesh as mere fear can never do . . . . You will understand that in such a situation there comes a place, a moment in time, beyond which even good intentions wither; a place where past and future lose all relevance.

She spoke then. "Go ahead; touch me. Reassure yourself." Her voice was the mere shadow of one, a vapor breathed on glass. I thought I detected a trace of accent—Italian, or Spanish perhaps.

"Who are you?" was all I could manage, an exhalation, an involuntary moan.

In answer she placed her right hand upon my thigh, two fingers against the shivering wing of my pelvic bone. Her touch made my stomach muscles twitch. In my mind I saw a clear image of that hand, fingers long and thin, tapered nails scarlet. She crooked her index finger so that the nail bit into my flesh.

"How did you get in here?" I asked. "Who are you? What do you want from me?"

"Shhh," she hissed, then nothing. A moment passed. Her hand slithered between my legs.

"I'm ready now," she breathed into my ear.

I rolled toward her, onto my side. All I could see was a silhouette against the pillow. Was it I who had drawn the curtains so tightly, banishing even the starlight?

"Do I know you?" I said. "Have we ever met?"

"You mustn't ask questions. It takes up too much time." She put her left hand upon my back and pulled me atop her. The past and the future disappeared.

"How much time do we have?" I asked.

Her heels touched one another at the base of my spine. "It's limited," she said.

I will not try to explain what it was like to make love to this shadow. Every possible description would demean it, would fall well short of truth. I can tell you only that the ineffable pleasure of it lasted almost till morning. During all those hours of darkness I felt no fatigue, not the least abatement of desire, until finally, after one of our numerous position changes—I would never have guessed so many possibilities existed—she pulled away from me and said, "I have to go to the bathroom now."

I said, "I wouldn't have thought that dream women need to do such things."

"Don't be foolish," she said. She kissed her fingertip and touched it to the center of my forehead, pushing me down again as I reached for her. "You'd better get some sleep."

A few moments later the light flickered on in the bathroom, then the door closed against it, leaving only a yellow thread of illumination upon the floor. I told myself to get up and turn on the bedroom lights so that I could have a look at her when she came out. But suddenly I was too tired to move, I could no longer keep my eyes open.

When the alarm woke me at 6:45 I imagined I had had a very erotic dream indeed. I was even able to dismiss the fact that the bathroom light was still burning. It was only when I stepped from the shower a half-hour later, and, drying myself, noticed the teeth marks on my buttock, and could discover no way I might have inflicted them myself, it was then I had to admit that my bed had been the playground for something other than a dream.

The following night I opened the curtains before retiring. I tied them back to let the moonlight flood my room. But when I awoke a few hours later, no longer alone in my bed, the curtains were drawn tight, the room as dark as a grave.

"Why don't you want me to look at you?" I asked her.

"Why do you need to?"

"What would it hurt?"

"Look with your fingers," she said. "Look with your mouth if you must, and your tongue. Look with your skin. Get inside me . . . deeper . . . deeper still. There; now look. What do you see? Look at me from the inside out."

On the third night I left a nightlight burning beside the bed. The room was, of course, pitch black when I awoke a few minutes after three AM. What awakened me was her weight upon my hips. She sat straddling me, leaning down, her hair forming a tent around our faces so that I could feel on mine the rose-scented vapors of her breath.

"You're playing games with me," she said.

"I'm not. I just need to see you, to have a glimpse of you. Just once."

She laid something against my neck then, something smooth and hot which, as she rolled it lightly over the carotid artery, I was able to identify as the bulb from the nightlight.

"These tricks won't do you any good," she said.

"I'm obsessed with you," I explained. "Every waking hour, you're all I can think about. It's impossible to concentrate, I'm falling behind in my work, my boss asked me today if I was coming down with something."

She laughed softly. "Maybe you are."

"If I could form a picture of you in my mind," I told her, "and put a name to that picture, it would be different, don't you see? Thinking about you wouldn't be so exhausting if I could put a face to all the other wonderful images I have of you."

Her breasts, for example, which I had reached up to hold, their weight heavy and solid in my hands, two wondrous handfuls of bloodwarm flesh—these I could picture all too clearly in my mind. Her hands, feet, the turn of her ankles, the taut musculature of her arching back—all these were as vivid to me when I touched them as if I were gazing at them in full sunlight. Her cascading hair, her earlobes, armpits, the thin scar that stretched like wire across her abdomen, just below the navel. All these <u>parts</u> I could vividly envision, but only singly, only as a fragment of a shadowy whole. I could hold in my mind a picture of only what I was touching at that moment. Her face alone reflected no light into my fingers, no lingering impression. Half a second after lifting my hand from her face, I could not tell you whether her lips were full and sensuous or as dry as matchsticks. Even now I have no idea if her nose is aquiline or pert, her eyes round or almond-shaped.

She ground her hips atop me. "You haven't gotten down to the deep places yet," she said.

Involuntarily, it seemed, I thrust harder. But she did not control my mind. "Maybe you should find somebody else to torment."

She pressed the light bulb against my neck until the thin glass burst. She then held the bare filament, that tiny stiff spear, against the corner of my eye. "You had better satisfy me tonight," she said. "All this talking has worked up an appetite."

My hands flew over her like ravenous bats.

On the final night before my wife returned, I awoke as usual not long after three, having found it impossible, despite my efforts, to remain awake past eleven. But even though I had fallen asleep in a living room chair, I awoke in my bed, unclothed. I was immediately aware, however, that no one lay beside me. I touched the mattress; it was cold. A mixture of relief and desperate fear shuddered through me. With the next breath I inhaled the scent of roses. I could see nothing, but my eyes were drawn to the foot of the bed, for I could feel her standing there, watching me.

Surreptitiously I slid my hand under the pillow and reached for the flashlight I had secreted there the day before. It was gone. Immediately a beam of light seared my eyes. It was painfully bright yet I could not look away from it. And never have I known the illumination from a flashlight to burn with such heat. I now understand what a deer or some other innocent creature must feel when it is pinned in the blaze of oncoming headlights and made to stand still for its own destruction.

"You haven't been working very hard to make me happy," she said.

"I'm a curious man. I'm sorry."

"No, you're not at all curious, except in a very limited way. If you were truly curious, you'd have discovered a more creative way to go about revealing me."

"I can't concentrate," I said. "You've fragmented my thoughts. You're ruining me."

"Get out of bed."

I would have protested, but she flicked the flashlight beam to the left, and I, as if tethered to it, moved too. In this way she drew me to the foot of the bed. She then lay on her back with her feet hooked behind my ankles. She brought me forward until I was standing between her knees.

"Put your hands behind your head," she instructed.

I did so, but complained. "I need to be able to touch you."

"You're being punished. Tonight you work blind."

"This will have to be our last night," I told her. "My wife returns tomorrow. Let's make tonight special, can't we?"

"Not another word out of you. Come forward now." She raised her legs, crossed her ankles behind my back, and dragged me into her.

She held me like this for the remainder of the night. As long as the flashlight blazed in my eyes, I could not resist. My body moved of its own accord; or rather, against its own will, a tortured machine. My fingers chaffed against the back of my own neck; my knees were skinned raw on the edge of the mattress. Her heels pounded my kidneys, her fingernails stabbed my thighs. I felt certain that the unrelenting light was scarring my retinas, blinding me forever, but even so I could not turn away. The pleasure was more exquisite than the punishment.

Finally, it must have been five AM by then, she tightened her legs around me and jerked me closer. Without warning she extinguished the flashlight. The instant the light went out, my orgasm hit me like a hundred-foot ocean wave, an icy angry wave that drove me headlong toward the sunless bottom, ten fathoms deep, so deep I did not think I would ever emerge from it, only to come up gasping, shivering, chilled to the bone.

She, now standing beside the bed, gazed down on me. She placed the flashlight in my hand, but my fingers were too limp to close around it, and the flashlight thudded to the floor.

She leaned over and kissed me lightly on the cheek. "Go to sleep now," she said. "Try not to dream of anything foolish." And she left me in darkness, still gasping for air.

My wife came home exhausted from her week of haggling and buying. Fortunately she was too weary to remark of or even notice my wan appearance. We shared a microwave dinner of frozen tortellinis in pesto sauce, a bottle of Beaujolais, and an hour of unmemorable television. We went to bed atypically early and, another irregularity, almost immediately turned our backs to one another and fell asleep.

My first response when I was later awakened was one of panic. "Don't worry," I heard whispered in my left ear. "She's sound asleep."

"Please, just go away. Are you trying to kill me?"

My wife mumbled something.

"If you talk, you'll wake her. Come on, I'm ready now. I've been thinking about it all day."

"I don't have the strength," I said.

My wife moaned again and rolled onto her back.

"You'd better keep quiet. Your fear is making a lot of noise."

I resolved to fight her, but my resolve lasted only as long as it took for her hands to slide down my stomach, the time it took her lips to find my mouth. Everything about her was warm now, as vaguely fragrant as a single rose.

"I won't be unkind," she said as she wriggled beneath me. "But you mustn't talk. Talk only with your hands and your body now. I'll hear everything you say."

I began slowly, cautiously, with my eyes on my wife. Strangely, I could see her rather clearly. In fact as the night progressed my wife became all too clear to me, as if her very skin were aglow with a gauzy illumination.

It did not take long for me to abandon my caution. The racing of my blood was the only signal I heeded. Even when my wife began to move beside me, moaning quite audibly now, her legs spread so that the left one lay crossed over mine, even this somehow aroused me more, that she, celibate for over a week now, was finding release in an erotic dream.

But if hers was a dream it was unlike any I had witnessed before. She cast aside the blanket and slept with her knees raised, sometimes one or both feet crooked high in the air. Her hips bucked the mattress as violently as did those of the woman beneath me. How both women's shrieks and groans kept from waking my wife, I cannot comprehend.

When it dawned on me finally that my wife was not dreaming—not unless my lover, too, was a dream—I felt a bottomless sadness, a profound loss. I thought of crying out to my wife, of waking her and pulling her to me, of doing anything that might dislodge these shadows and free us from their hold. But before the thought could become act, a rose-scented whisper warmed my ear.

"Don't do anything foolish," it said.

I haven't touched my wife in over two months now. She has yet to complain of my negligence. When awake, we are, or try to be, considerate of one another's need for quietude. But we are both looking rather strained these days, almost haggard. My coworkers repeatedly inquire of my health. I am certain to lose my job soon.

Somehow, without enough of a struggle, my wife and I have let this thing divide us, this thing that never satisfies and is never sated. We should have fought harder against it, should have looked away, should have looked to one another instead of avoiding each other's eyes. We offered only token resistance and have allowed it to become too strong. It has trampled the soul of our love. We are helpless now. We are lost.

At home, my wife and I retire for the evening as soon as the sun is down. We keep the curtains tightly drawn. We ask no questions of each other or ourselves. We demand no answers. One or both of us is surely mad.

I sat motionless for a long time, waiting for Louisa Cecelia's response. Had she fallen asleep? The candles sputtered and cracked.

"Do you want to make love now?" she finally asked.

"You don't like it, do you?"

"I've heard a lot of stories, Devon."

I felt crushed. "Can you tell me what's wrong with it?"

I watched her finger and thumb caress a nipple. I watched the nipple harden.

"I don't know about that last line," I told her. "Should it be 'one or both of us is surely made' or 'one or both of us are surely mad'?"

Louisa Cecelia said, "I'm not a succubus."

"No, I know! I never meant . . . . I mean it's just a story."

"Do you think I'm evil?"

"God, no. I think you're . . . . I think you're beautiful."

"But you do feel evil for wanting me. Because I look like a child."

"There is some truth to that."

"But you look like a child to me," she said.

"I do?"

"A baby."

I laughed softly.

"So I'm the one who should feel bad, not you."

"I guess," I said, "when you look at it that way . . . ."

"So maybe I am evil."

I offered no reply, had none to offer. The flickering lights played over her skin, they cast a softly rippling illusion of golden scales, of fluidity and motion. I had the sensation of being on *The Egg* again, I could feel the ocean in my legs.

"You're afraid of the city, aren't you, Devon?"

The Egg dropped down into a trough between waves. "I don't think so," I said.

"It's in your story."

"Is it?"

"Are you afraid of me?"

"Is that in there too?"

"That and a lot more you don't know."

"Yes, well . . . . It's just a story."

"Art is the invisible mind made visible."

"It is?"

"Look around."

I squinted at the nearest shadowbox. In it were shards of green and amber glass shaped into a fractured sun. The sun shone on a small dented globe tilted dangerously on its axis, as if at any moment it might fall off and roll away. In another, what might have been a handful of shattered tempered glass from a windshield had become a star field, with below it another star field identical in design beneath a sheet of crinkled blue cellophane. And between the two a menagerie of disparate objects stacked like a staircase: a cell phone, a pad of neon yellow Post-It notes, a silver dollar, a floppy disk, a credit card, an empty prescription bottle.

My gaze moved from one candlelit box to the next. My mind strained to make sense of each one individually and all of them together but my mind felt as fragmented as her fractured sun. The dissonance dizzied me. The wind outside whistled through the eaves and made the wallboards creak. I could smell the ocean in that wind, the strawberry-scented wax. I think I might have lost consciousness for a moment or two but somehow remained standing. I remember the slow awareness that came to me as her hands undid my belt and opened my jeans and let them slide to the floor, I was leaning into her then, steadying myself against her. *The Egg* was heaving up and down in the waves.

Just as she pulled me forward and I tumbled onto the bed, a single thought filled my head. To call it a thought, however, is misleading; it was more of a sudden comprehension that hit me like a slap and lasted only as long. I suddenly perceived each one of her shadowboxes as, for example, a wind-gnarled tree clinging to a cliff's edge. That is, I perceived each shadowbox as an entity separate from the wall just as the tree is separate from the cliff, each a thing unto itself, but each shadowbox also an expression of the wall. And each wall, the room. The room the house. The house this island. And on and on. And, of course, somewhere in that equation, was Louisa Cecilia. But was she at the beginning of the equation or the end? And where and how did I fit in?

She giggled like a little girl.

My lips moved to form a question, but before they could, her mouth covered mine.

And so it continued. Throughout the first week of nightly visits our conversations were brief but they always left me winded and confused, as if I had raced to the top of a hill and found it different than the hill I had thought I was climbing, everything strange, the trees out of place, a few red pines where I had expected oaks, the horizon unfamiliar, an unfamiliar land in the distance. At the same time there was an airiness to this hill, which was in fact her bedroom, a spaciousness that contradicted the room's dimensions.

A strange lightness always came over me there, a sensation I still find difficult to describe. For one thing, every time I looked at the shadowboxes, some new detail that had previously eluded me became obvious. The Dungeness crab claw, for example, that reached down from an upper corner while, from the opposite bottom corner, a cardboard cut-out of a naked toddler, a boy, placed inside a paper boat, reached toward the claw.

"Is this a new one?" I asked.

"Is it new to you, Devon?"

"I don't remember seeing it before. But the rest of it—everything else in this shadowbox—I do."

"So is the difference in the thing perceived or in the perceiver?"

She dizzied me in more ways than one. Within minutes of entering her bedroom each night I felt half-drunk, and the more of her candlelit darkness I inhaled, the drunker I grew. By the time she wrapped her legs around me I felt like a swimmer adrift on a rolling sea, being carried by riptide to a distant unknown. Yet it was a sea that buoyed me up, held me safely afloat. A sea where jellyfish did not sting, where sharks swam below but did not attack.

If not for the lack of an incriminating scent—always the fragrance of strawberries—I would have sworn she was burning hashish.

And when I left her doll's house each morning, when I stepped out into the 3 AM night, I felt as sailors do when stepping ashore after a long voyage, as if the land itself is moving beneath them, gently heaving as the sea had not. It became my habit to make my way to the cliff where McDermott had tumbled, and there to lie down on a patch of grass, and find a stability again in the sea breeze washing over me, the thunderous waves pounding the rocks below.

Within an hour my senses would sharpen, my thoughts become clear. At those times it would seem I could hear the murmur of the darkness itself as it shared its secrets with the sea. The sea would then whisper to the sand, the sand to the rocks, the rocks to the earth, the earth to the grass. Then the grass would tickle my ear with a language I could not understand but heard like a humming song, wordless melody, and my heart would grow heavy with lightness, a condition impossible to understand until it has been experienced.

Strange thoughts sprang into my head. For example: *Grass understands bones better than bones understand themselves.* And each thought would spawn another. *How many bones have the meadows swallowed? How many bones have fed and flavored the grasses? So if a bone hopes to know itself it must first become the grass that feeds the cow that feeds the man whose flesh will fade and fall away and drop its bones into the grass.*

Familiar sights looked foreign to me. The lighthouse, the school, my old shoes, my own hands. I feared for my sanity. Yet was thrilled by the novelty of it all.

During the days that followed I did not go to the dock or to the fishing grounds with Jasper. He never once came looking for me, never called my apartment nor ventured up the stairs from The Sow's Ear. I stayed out of the bar, kept to myself, frequented only the unpeopled places. I ate little, drank no coffee or alcohol. Something else was sustaining me. Always there was the moan and rumble of the ocean in my ears. It sounded like a distant didgeridoo, full of melancholy and longing. It made me think of a father who was wandering the night, calling for his lost child, a child so long gone that he would be grown by now but even so the father's pain had not aged, the grief was still young and raw.

And always there were the cloud shadows, great adumbrations skimming over the water and the island like lone humpback whales gliding just beneath the surface. Always the terns and seagulls wheeling and hovering, white wings glinting like bone in the sun, cries as shrill as knives. Always there was the briny scent of the air, always the salt grit on my face. And always too there was the island wind, musky with the scent of the depths, and the wind that blew through my heart, such loneliness.

On the morning of the sixth day of my time with Louisa Cecelia I left the cliff face with another story burbling in my head. I had gazed across the ocean and imagined in the fog of dawn an old man setting out alone to make his day's catch. He was a man who had been cursed with bad luck all his life, or maybe just bad choices. He became clearer to me as I walked back to my apartment. There I wrote until four, went through the story a half dozen times. Then I slept until dark. Then rose and showered and carried my story to Louisa Cecelia.

"This one is called 'A Change of Course'."

"Of course," she said.

And I read:

> Old, sore, and stiff. As brittle as an ice-crusted mooring line. That was how Quincas the fisherman saw himself, how he felt. As bumpy as an old potato. His skin had more wens than a toad had warts. He was an ugly man, and he knew it. Nobody but his wife could stand the sight of him.
>
> And Quincas, in turn, could not look upon his wife without flinching. Although only moderately unattractive herself, she was a shrill woman, stingy with everything but her insults. She and Quincas had no children, because, he believed, his sperm shrank from her in terror, ran out the way they had come, preferring a soggy death on a cold mattress to a lifetime of admonishment and shame. Quincas had been drunk the night he married her, half a century ago, in New Bedford, Massachusetts. The next morning, after she had jabbed him awake to announce that they were man and wife, he got drunk again.

For fifty odd years, then, he had loved going out in his fishing boat *Aurora*, an old wooden side trawler, loved rolling along between troughs of waves in the brisk North Atlantic, dragging his net across the ocean floor in search of codfish, haddock, and yellowtail flounder. On good days and bad he loved the weather on his face, welcomed wind and sun and rain and snow, the blasting heat and the pricking cold, and he was always sad when the time came to return within range of his wife's vile tongue.

For fifty odd years—the odd times were the nights, which he spent at home—he had loved the sea, had felt at ease there, comfortable even with the wens that blossomed like pale nubby mushrooms on his hairless head, his shoulders and his back. My barnacles, he thought of them, and not without some pride, except when another human being was near enough to stare at him and grimace in revulsion.

But lately it seemed as if he and the sea had had a falling out. For weeks now he had pulled nothing from his net but junk—discarded tires, plastic bags full of garbage. Last week a computer monitor had tumbled from his net. It shattered when he dumped it onto the deck.

In his younger days Quincas had worked as a deckhand on other men's boats, but as time went by he grew disenchanted with their company. When the 31-foot *Aurora* came up for sale, he scrounged and scraped, even scavenged for cans and soda bottles along the roadsides, until he had managed to put together a down payment. Adjustments were made to the equipment so that he could handle everything on his own, a smaller net, a winch and pulley he could operate from the wheelhouse, and his had been a solitary life ever since.

He loved to hear the deep-throated whine and whir of the winch's motor when a heavy net came in. A productive haul might invoke from him at least three exultant Good Christ Almighties. But those days seemed long past. His epithets now were muttered curses. The groundfish stocks were depleted. The government, under pressure from recreational longliners and environmental groups, had closed off the best fisheries and shortened seasons to a few desperate weeks. And here it was October already, the height of the cods' inshore migration run. But where were the fish?

Quincas often told himself that if he had had a son, his son would be a man now, and they would work the *Aurora* together. Then if the net came in empty, his son would tell him not to worry, next time you'll be cursing to high heaven, and they would drink a bottle of beer together, dark heavy beer with foam as thick as spindrift. And maybe his son would talk about the women he knew, just explicitly enough that the old man would remember what it was like when that bulging burn in the pants drained a man of all reason.

His son—Leo; or maybe Adam—would be good-looking, a real ladies' man. Too smart to settle down with a shrewish wife. But he would not blame the old man for his own moment of weakness, a moment fifty odd years long. The old man was too ugly to have done any better.

Unfortunately, there was no son. No child at all. The old man's seed swam in the wrong direction. What kind of son could you expect from that?

So the old man worked alone, same as always. For the past three weeks the net had always come in empty but for the junk. Oh, a keeper here and there maybe, something for his supper. But no money fish. Nothing to fill the hold.

And now that the old man thought of it—he had more time to think than he liked—the word *empty* summed up his life in a nutshell. His boat was all but falling apart, for there was no money for repairs. He could not squeeze another nickel of credit from acquaintance or stranger. His house was a shack, cold and sterile. There had never been anything left after expenses to put in the bank. He didn't even own a car. What did he have to show for seventy-three years of living? Even his cowardly sperm had dried up—or so he assumed, having had little cause in recent years to inquire of their condition.

It was time now to check the net again, but why bother? It will be empty, he told himself, same as always. He stared at the dark sea, black in its October coldness, frothy in its late afternoon chill. The wind was sharp with minute pricks of rain, wet needles too small to see but painful nonetheless. The sky too was gray, just one long sunless cloud. And yet . . . it was beautiful. Christ, it *was* beautiful. All that beautiful gray emptiness, it was too damn beautiful to bear.

He cut the engine, hit the button to start the winch, and left the wheelhouse. He stood with his hands on the cold starboard rail, where his son's hands should have been, and he held his ugly face to the wind. And he let the icy rain prick the tears from his eyes.

Stupid, he told himself. Stupid and useless. What good are tears? Those few had been the first to pass his eyes since . . . since the morning he awoke to find himself married.

You can cry a bucket of tears, he told himself, an ocean, but will anything change? You will be more dried up than ever, more emptied out, but other than that?

Crazy old fool. Shame on you.

When the pitch of the winch's whine shifted higher he leaned into the wheelhouse and shut off the motor. Then crossed to the port side, where the net would be hanging over the hold. Hanging empty, he told himself. Hanging limp as my dick.

But the net was not empty. And in those moments before his eyes could cut through the gray air and focus on what hung thrashing in the net, he thought *Dolphin? Shark? Baby pilot whale?* Even when he saw it, saw her, it, whatever it was, his brain fought recognition. His mind denied the evidence, sorted through every strange thing his net had ever produced, living or dead, mechanical or corporeal, plastic, wood, rubber, metal, animal or vegetable, evil or good.

In the end there was no denying what he saw. Still, she was unlike any mermaid he had ever read about or seen in the movies. But then, he hadn't been to the movies since Carole Lombard died, and the only books he read were the same three *National Geographics* that had been in the Seamen's Rescue League Hall since 1961. Maybe if he had kept up-to-date she wouldn't appear so foreign to him. Leo—no, in this case Adam—would know what to do in a situation like this. As for the old man, he could only gasp and blink, a dumb fish himself.

She was not much bigger than a child, a girl. Her tail was not emerald green as a mermaid's should have been, nor noticeably scaled, but as silvery as a dolphin's, as smooth and iridescently mottled as a seabed of polished marble. Her belly was a lighter gray than her back, where between the sharp wings of her shoulder blades stood a short stiff dorsal fin. She had breasts of a sort, barely larger than dusty gray rosebuds, the nipples hard tiny nubs. She was most definitely a fish, and yet . . . well . . . she most definitely was not a fish. Her arms were long and slender, the fingers webbed. From forearms to ribcage stretched translucent membranes as thin and fragile-looking as sugar-glazed rice paper—pectoral fins, the old man supposed; as on a flying fish. She was obviously a fish, and yet . . . well . . . .

Her face. That was not the face of a fish. Not the eyes, nose, mouth, not the head of any fish he had ever seen before. She was beautiful. Christ, she *was* beautiful. She was a child, a girl. And yet, a woman. A fish. Christ. Good Christ Almighty.

Her hair was very short, and red. But not red. Not even hair, for that matter. Fuzz, but very thick. Thick and very short. And not quite red. Pale. Nearly transparent. Salmon colored. Beautiful.

Her eyes, green. Kelp green. They blinked very slowly. The gills below her jawline blinked too. Gasped. Opened and closed, opened and closed.

She hung there looking at him and never made a sound. His hand trembling, his entire body trembling, shivering, shuddering, he leaned toward her, he put out one gnarled finger, one thick ugly potato root, the nail ragged, black, unlike any other human fingernail he had ever seen, and gently, delicately, he pushed it through the net, he touched it to her cheek. She blinked. Her gills silently gasped, opened and closed. She hung there looking at him and never made a sound.

"Jesus," he said, "you're like a miracle or something. What in God's name are you?"

She looked at him and blinked. She didn't make a sound. Maybe she couldn't. Maybe she didn't want to. He wished he knew what to think, what to do. He wished he had a son to help him out here.

What he did know finally was that a fish, any fish, even a fishgirl, would die out of water. Fish have gills. So did this girlfish. In fact her eyes looked sleepy already. Clouding. Her gills fluttered.

He did not want to dump her in the hold. But he did not want to leave her hanging high and dry either. He wanted her wet for her own sake, and, for his, in a position that he could study her. As he hurried toward the flare locker, he called out through the pricking rain. "I'm sorry for staring," he said, and threw open the metal lid. "But I can't help looking at you." He dragged out the yellow life raft, kicked it open, jerked on the cord attached to the C02 canisters. Within seconds the raft was fully inflated.

"I mean . . . Christ," he said, and heaved a five gallon plastic bucket overboard. He leaned over the rail then and reclaimed the rope tied to the bucket's handle, pulled up the overflowing container, splashed the water into the raft. "It's just . . . I don't know," he said, and threw the bucket out again, "I don't know," and reeled it in, "you're so strange," and splashed the water into the raft, "but so beautiful."

Soon there were two inches of water in the bottom of the raft. Not enough, but enough for the moment. He dragged the raft as close as possible beneath the net, then pulled the net lopsided so that it hung over the raft. He pulled the pin to open the metal door at the bottom of the net but held the door in place. "I'm going to touch you now," he said. "I've got to put you in the raft. In the water. You'll feel better there. You'll get your breath back. So please don't squirm, I wouldn't want to drop you. Please forgive my hands. They're a mess, I know, but they're the only ones I've got."

It was difficult to hold the net in place while easing open the door, and while trying to catch her from falling out. But he was a strong man and used to pain and he did not even flinch when the door's metal frame cut into his arm. He thought for sure that she would squirm away from him when he laid his callous-encrusted mitts on her, on her sleek and mucous-slick body, but she didn't make a sound, didn't pull away. "All right, you understand," he said. "Here goes."

He slipped his wet hands beneath her, one at the hip, the other at the shoulder. Her skin was warm; he nearly moaned aloud at the touch. As he took her weight into his arms and knelt toward the raft his knees snapping audibly. Free from the net she rolled toward him, into his embrace. One hand came up to touch the back of his neck, the wet warm fingertips against his bumpy skin.

"Christ," he moaned, "oh Christ," because his heart was racing so wildly, so wild with sweet and violent pain, racing not because of her weight but because of something else, something else.

"You're a sea angel," he said, too embarrassed to turn his face to hers when she was so near, "a special kind of angel who lives in the sea."

Her fingers pushed harder on the back of his neck. He looked at her then and saw that her eyes were nearly closed. "Oh God no, don't. Don't. Hold on. Here we go, into the water, hold on. You'll be all right now, you'll be fine. Here we go, here we are. Into the raft."

He told himself that there was a quicker way to revive her, a surer way, just put her back where she belongs, give her back to the sea. But he could not do it. He had never seen such beauty in all his life. Had never felt so blessed. How could he refuse such a gift?

Tenderly he lay her on her side in the middle of the raft. She rolled facedown in the shallow water. As he drew his hands from beneath her his fingertips grazed the tiny breasts and he felt his chest cave in around his heart, he felt the boat pitch and fall away. Then he was holding only to the raft, and everything steadied again. He stood and went to the rail and threw out the plastic bucket, then spent the next fifteen minutes moving the ocean onto his deck.

"Your air," he said as he laid the water over her, "this is your air. The air you breathe, the air you fly in. It's your heaven, your clouds. It's sweet to breathe, isn't it? Good Christ, you're beautiful. You are, you're so beautiful I can't even think of anything to compare you with. It makes me feel stupid, because I don't have any words for it. It makes me feel like I've had too much wine to think straight. Not enough to make me sad, not that much. Four, maybe five glasses worth. The way I get then, when everything seems wonderful. Seems perfect. It takes twice that much to make me sad. So sad I just want to climb onto my boat and keep sailing into the sun forever and let it burn me away and never go back. But that's not how I feel now, seeing you. I feel happy-drunk. Like I can't think straight. And don't even care."

Finally it occurred to him that for every bucketful of water he dumped into the raft, a bucketful sloshed out and onto the deck. The sea angel was lying on her back now, on her right shoulder and dorsal fin, four inches of dusky water atop her face as she gazed up at him. "Are you smiling?" he asked. He stood there with the empty bucket in hand, his trousers and shoes soaked with cold water, and he felt wave after wave of happiness swell through him.

"I'm a real eyeful, ain't I?" he said. He tossed the bucket out of the way and lowered himself to the wet slippery deck, sat gingerly in the cold spilled sheen. "Don't quite know what to make of me, do you? Well, I'm just an ugly old man, that's it. I'm about as ugly as ugly gets."

Her wide-finned tail skimmed the raft's rubber bottom, swishing back and forth. Occasionally it broke the surface and slapped down again, freshening her air. Particles of kelp and other organic matter drifted past her eyes. She blinked docilely but continued to smile, what he thought was a smile, what he hoped, her lips pale and thin and mouth closed, and the old man told himself she's getting stronger now, she'll be all right, everything's going to be fine.

For a while then she rolled her head away from him to survey what she could of the boat. "That's the wheelhouse," he told her, following her eyes. "I can steer from there."

She rolled her head to the right, took it all in. Then she looked to the left.

"It's not much, is it?" he said. "If she holds together another year or two, that'll be fine. I probably won't last much longer than that myself. Then my wife can sell the fittings and equipment and go live with her sister in Nantucket. That'll be the happiest day of her life, I guess." He grinned, showing his strong white teeth, the only aspect of his visage he didn't consider repugnant. She smiled and did not look away.

"You'd never guess by looking at me that I could have a beautiful son, would you?" he said. "But I do. His name is Adam. He smiles at the girls in town and just like that their hearts break, he's so beautiful. And strong! He's over six feet tall, two hundred pounds, and I've seen him throw his own weight in ice over his back as if it was a bag of feathers."

She blinked slowly, her kelp green eyes so bright and clear.

"Him and me worked this boat together ever since he was a boy," the old man told her. "But a while back I started having trouble keeping up with him, he was doing his share of work and part of mine too. So I helped him to get started on his own. I helped him get set up. Now he's got a beauty of a boat, a forty-footer. He's got a two-man crew under him. He's making money hand over fist."

He looked into her eyes and saw the trust there and he knew that everything he had told her was true. For the moment it was all true and he had not made any of it up. It was wonderful to know this, it made him as happy as he had ever been. He looked into the sky and saw faint stars shining through the blanket of gray, a faint moon made gauzy and soft by the clouds. The rain had stopped and the wet cold now felt clean on his face. The air was clean and cold and he had never felt better.

A prize like this, he told himself, such a rarity, such a gift, it has to be a blessing, there's no other way to explain it. Her beauty would make him famous, erase his ugliness, turn his ugliness into a beauty of its own. The moment he showed her to anyone else he would become a celebrity, instantly immortal. In fact he felt immortal just gazing upon her. Immortal and, in a disturbing way, insignificant. Others would try to take her from him. He would have to fight like a wild man. But he would, he would fight to the death if necessary, because she could make anything possible for him. *Anything*.

When he looked down again he thought the stars had fallen into the raft and were swimming atop her. The tiny photoplanktons twinkled and shone, orange and gold. He dipped a gnarled hand into the cold water and delicately stirred the stars, rearranged heaven. She slipped her hand into his and drew his calloused knuckles to her cheek.

In this position the old man fell asleep. He dreamed he lay beside her, the ocean rocking their bodies together, the ocean wrapped around them and keeping them joined, his body as fluid and buoyant as hers. But he had no gills and his breathing was labored, he was unable to suck enough oxygen from the water. Even so, he thought he could hold on a while longer, stay with her, see it through. He would rather drown than disappoint her now. In his dream her lips were pressed to his neck, fingers gripping his shoulder blades. Her wings enveloped him, made them indivisibly one as his thighs tightened around her, his legs crossed at the ankle around her tail, pulling, drawing them tighter together as she began to quiver against him, pale mouth open upon his neck. Then *Oh Christ!* he cried and he died for an instant, he disappeared completely in the sweet black water of unconsciousness. Then gradually he returned, his body bits of plankton coalescing, one dim star, fading light, and he came awake and said "Oh Christ" again, but differently this time.

He opened his eyes and saw that she was watching him. He felt ashamed, ugly, a repulsive old man. He drew his hand out of the cold water. He looked away from her, he stood stiffly, shivering, and went to sit alone where her eyes could no longer find him.

In an ugly world, Quincas the fisherman told himself, we love beauty so much that we destroy it. In this manner we destroy ourselves. So how could her beauty make him immortal? She couldn't. Nothing could. And the old man, ugly as he was, miserable as he was, grudgingly admitted to himself that he wanted to live forever.

It was nearly dawn by the time he maneuvered the boat back near the spot where the fishgirl had been scooped from the sea. There he killed the engine and held his breath for a moment. He listened to the silence, which was not silent at all, but full, complete, brimming with the slap of waves against the hull, the smell and taste of the sea and night and the fog-wrapped stars and the disappearing moon. Then he filled his lungs with this beautiful emptiness, he drank it in until he was happy-drunk and brave.

Moving gingerly, wanting to avoid even the slightest creaking of the boards, he went to the gunwale and worked loose the removable section of sidewall, creating an opening four feet wide. He stowed this board out of the way, then tiptoed to the raft.

Her eyes were closed. Her tail skimmed lightly back and forth, and in the gentle currents of this movement her hand seemed to flutter, slender webbed fingers like tiny wings unfurled and riding the air. Her salmon-colored hair waved like silken grass in a breeze. Christ, she's beautiful, he thought. Good Christ Almighty.

Bending at the knees and back he slipped his thick fingers beneath the braided rope that encircled the raft. Delicately he brought his hands toward his hips, easing out the slack. The rope grew taut. He filled his lungs with a slow steady breath and at the same time moved his left foot backward, felt the ropy muscles in his forearm tighten and burn, and he set the raft in motion.

With the first scrape of the raft across the deck she opened her eyes. She looked up at him, bewildered. Her tail thrashed up and slapped down, she rolled from side to side.

Tears streamed from his face. "I'm not hurting you," he told her. "Don't worry. I wouldn't hurt you." Hunched over, aching, he pulled harder now, faster toward the open rail. Water splashed out of the raft, gray chilling water on his feet and hands.

He finally reached the gunwale. Still he could not look at her, could not allow it, a single glance would defeat him. As he hurried past her to the other side of the raft she reached out, her trembling hand grazed his leg. The touch so weakened him that he feared he could not finish the job. Obviously she did not understand.

He knelt at her head and pushed hard on the inflated tubing. The raft slid through the opening. As its stern dipped toward the water the bow tipped up, slowly up, its water draining out, stars splashing into heaven, and she rolled onto her stomach and reached out with both hands and tried to interlock her fingers behind his neck, but her grip was awkward and wet and she slid away from him, her winghands fluttered across his cheeks, angel wings outstretched, and she slipped away, over the edge, out of the raft, into the dark liquid sky of his dream.

He heard the splash. On his knees he slid forward. The raft was floating upside down, drifting away, a pale yellow cloud scudding across the dark sky. He believed he saw her watching him from just below the surface of the dark water, those kelp green eyes. But this vision lasted only a moment, and when it was gone and the water calmed again, he doubted that any of it had been real.

And this is the way with blessings, isn't it, he thought. The leap of a dolphin. A waterspout shimmering in the sun. To leave nothing behind but a gasp of wonder.

After a while he could no longer see the yellow raft. The sun, swollen and red as it sat upon the ocean, streamed warming light over the rail. He felt it on his face, tightening the skin, stinging his eyes. He sat there until the gray of dawn burned away.

Later he went to the wheelhouse and started the engine. He held it in neutral a few moments, enjoying the resonant growl. Then he pushed the throttle forward and aimed *Aurora* into the sun. He stared unblinking at the brightness until he went blind from it, saw nothing but an ocean of flames, a universe ablaze. Then, grinning broadly, showing his fine white teeth, he spun the wheel hard, swung the boat around in a wide looping turn that raised a splendid wake. With the sun at his back now, burning his neck and shoulders and his bare knobby skull, the hold as empty as always, Quincas the fisherman headed for home.

❦

"It's a happier story this time," she said.

"I suppose it is."

"Are you a happier man now?"

She looked so lovely lying there, I could not help but smile. "I suppose I am."

She watched me as I undressed. She watched my hands moving down the buttons of my shirt, watched the belt pulled open, shoes pried off, socks tossed aside, jeans shed like a snakeskin outgrown. I eased myself atop her and rested on my knees between her legs, our bodies touching here and there, just touching, skin kissing skin.

"So what is different now?"

In the touch and heat and pull of her flesh I had already forgotten our brief conversation. I drew back and looked at her.

"You still live where you live," she said. "You still have the same job, except that you haven't been going to it, which means you've been making no money. You are still what you are. So what do you have to be happier about?"

Had the look on her face been the least bit scornful, had there been even a glint of disdain in her eyes, I might have burst into tears, so suddenly undone did I feel. But she regarded me as a consoling mother would, and though I viewed myself as stupid and ugly in her eyes, she raised a hand to stroke my cheek.

"A succubus and a mermaid," she said. "A young man and an old man. What other stories do you have to tell?"

"None," I told her.

"No more?"

"I feel so empty now."

She raised herself and kissed my mouth. She tasted of mango, exotic and sweet.

"Roll over, dear boy. Let me help you out of yourself a while."

Despite her ministrations, despite the warmth of blood that brought physical response, my thoughts remained dark. I thought of McDermott and Litwiler. Had this woman whose mouth was moving over me now in ways impossible to ignore been responsible for their deaths? She lifted her head for a moment and smiled at me. Could she read my thoughts?

"You need to let go, Devon."

"Let go of what?"

"Sometimes a man can lose himself in a woman's tenderness."

"And then?"

"Sometimes that lost man can find himself there."

I began to relax. I focused my thoughts on the slow sensuous movements of her hand.

"But sometimes what he finds," she said, "is that there is nothing there to find."

More nights passed. Even now I do not know how many. They were all like a single night to me, with periods between that were lit by misted sunlight, diffusing fog, and on occasion a glare of sun that stung my eyes. These intervening periods were, as I said, spent alone. Something was changing in me but I could not have said what, I only knew that I did not care to discuss it with anyone. One day I watched a striped chipmunk for two hours, followed it from tree to tree, studied the way it dug for seeds in the grass, how it hulled the seeds, chewed and swallowed and went searching again. One afternoon was spent matching my own breath with the ocean's. Another day matching our heartbeats, systolic, diastolic, blood rushing in, blood surging out.

All of one morning I sat on a spit of land while the sea spray bathed my face and I watched as individual grains of sand were pulled into the water, stolen away again, replaced and whisked away. I wondered where that sand had come from originally, where it was going, and at times I could sense myself being drawn away with it. It occurred to me that the spit of land I was sitting on had once been a mountain, once a billion shells now ground to tiny pearls, once the bones of a thousand mastodons, once the cave walls where callused hands wet with blood were pressed, once the world as someone knew it, now sand I hardly knew at all.

In the flap of a heron's wings I saw the grace of muscle and feather and bone, I saw the freedom and the grace I lacked. The physicality of nature fell upon my senses and became metaphor.

On another day I sat in the abandoned lighthouse, sat on the dirt and glass-littered floor beside the shattered light, and brooded about the stories I had written. I had felt such pride in their completion but was now ashamed of that pride. Like a leaf caught in a dust devil I went round and round between wanting to write another story and vowing to never write again. What good were mere stories? What good were mere words?

In the beginning there was the Word. What did that mean? That God created the universe by articulating the idea? By writing or speaking the universe into being?

Heidegger said that "only the word grants being to a thing." But man is not God. Man does not write life into being. On the other hand, by witnessing and participating in life, does he then give it human meaning? Does he then include himself in the mystery of life? If that is the case, then the articulation of the experience, the word, is not for life's sake but man's sake. Otherwise he remains a mute and dumb outsider.

No, words do not awaken the world into being. But can they awaken the man to the inexpressible being of the world?

One night I stepped into Louisa Cecelia's bedroom and immediately sensed a difference, some odd vibration in the air, though she was lying as always near the center of her bed, poised on a hip and elbow as she watched me come inside, her robe open to reveal the slender smooth curve of hip I knew so well by then that I could close my eyes at any time of day or night and experience it again. I unbuttoned my shirt as I crossed to her, but moved haltingly this time, sniffing the air like a meerkat.

"Oranges," I finally said.

She smiled. "I changed the candles."

Just then one of the three candles atop her dresser crackled and flickered out. "Would you light that, Devon? The matches are there."

I crossed to the dresser and picked up the book of matches. *The Sow's Ear* was printed on its cover. *Come make a Hogg of yourself.* I was about to remark to Louisa Cecelia than in all my many days and nights in the tavern I had never once seen her inside, but as I lit the candle, then raised the match to blow it out, my gaze was caught by the shadowbox hanging on the wall directly above the dresser. The box was new, twice as long as it was high, the kind of white pine box in which a pair of wine bottles might be shipped. In the lower left corner of the box sat a seagull's egg. A chick's head and neck protruded from a hole in the egg, as if the chick had just then poked its way through and was struggling to climb out. Next to it was a smiling Ken doll, naked, standing on a small rock. His left foot was poised on the very right edge of the rock, his right foot raised as if he were about to step off into a void. The last object, filling the right side of the box from top to bottom, was a flimsy strip of white cloth somehow suspended—by fishing line, I guessed—so as to appear to hang in mid-air. The bottom half of the cloth hung free and moved with the heat rising off the candles, but the upper half was stretched taut, which created the impression that it was reaching for another seagull egg, this one whole and suspended from the upper right corner of the box.

The three figures created a progression of sorts, and an unsettling one at that, though I could not have explained why I felt so uneasy. "It's interesting," I said.

"Is it?"

"What exactly does it mean?"

"It doesn't mean. It is."

Did she know that she was paraphrasing Archibald MacLeish?

"Come lay with me," she said.

I was torn between wanting to stand there and puzzle out the shadowbox's suggestion and wanting to please Louisa Cecelia. I chose the latter. As always, her body soon bewitched me and I attuned myself to her pleasure, falling in love with the blush that spread across her chest and up her neck, becoming fixated on the quivering of her hamstring, the way her toes tightened into a curl. Hours later, after her pleasure had swelled and crested several times, the last time sent me racing skyward into a clamorous and fiery height only to drift slowly down, down, undulating down to make the softest of landings atop her.

For a few minutes I forgot all about her shadowboxes, all about my stories. I wallowed in the sweet exhaustion. I rolled onto my back, stretched out beside her, and yawned.

She said, "Are you yawning your life away, Devon?"

Her voice held no tone of scorn yet the words hit me like the sharpest of rebukes. I struggled to think of some way to redeem myself, to prove myself worthy of her. But what could I say? Over the past many days I had spent nearly every hour of darkness in her company. I had abandoned my brother, earned no money, could pay no rent for the month. I had dawdled away the daylight by staring at the ocean, contemplating rocks, studying dewdrops. What a foolish man I had been.

I eased out of her bed, found my clothes and slipped them on. All the while I was hoping she would call me back to bed. But she did not even roll over to look at me. I slinked out of her room, hungry for at least a sleepy "Goodnight." But no words were spoken.

I intended that morning to meet Jasper at *The Egg* before he set off at six a.m., to work like a madman all that day and the next and every next that remained, gutting and cleaning every fish that dropped out of the net, anticipating and fulfilling his every need before he even conceived of them. But at shortly after five, rather than sit at my table and watch the clock tick, I laid the legal pad in front of me and, meaning only to doodle away another half hour, picked up the pen.

When I finished writing I had three full pages of lines, most of them crossed out but with thirty-three lines intact. I had written a poem.

I felt both happy and ashamed. It was now 8:45. Jasper was out past the Shoals by now, dragging the net through the Dwyers, hoping for a change of luck. If luck came to him today, it would be none of my doing. What a sorry ass brother and mate I was.

Still, I had written a poem. I was ashamed of it, yes. But I loved it too.

That night, like a little boy eager to impress his teacher, I read the poem to Louisa Cecelia. "It's called 'Flying Fish,'" I told her.

> When winter comes and all the boxes
> have been knocked together, filled and
> left to weather, rot and fall apart,
> be picked apart by all the crabs
> and crows and termite-days,
> I will live on a spit of land just past
> the boulder field where philosophers play,
> on a slender sandy reach of land
> thrown up for just a gasp or sigh of time,
> a narrow peninsula shaped like a tongue
> in the tidal zone between hard and soft,
> static and fluid, grounding and launch,
> where ebb meets flow and soul meets flesh,
>   and there I will have the thrashing water at my door,
> a water too angry to freeze,
> no mere lake silenced into gray monotony,
> no river's tongue choked by ice and
> numbed to mumbling.
> I want the waves to rattle my frosted windows.

I want the creak and slam to heave my walls.

Yes set my house on the ocean's edge
where the breakers will shove me hard against
the sandy bank, where the tide will slap
and seize and drag me toward the depths,
where the undertow will push me down
to charcoal waters where the creatures have
no eyes and see with skin.

Yes set my house on the ocean's edge
where the pressure of the deep unseen
will mold my feet into flippers,
compress my lungs into gills,
and where the world high above waits
but a leap and a splash away.

I told her, "It's about living on the water."
  "No, it's not," she said.
  "It's not?"
  "You already live on the water."
  "Well, on the land near the water."
  "Though in truth neither," she said.
  I cocked my head at her.
  "In truth, you hardly exist."
  I cannot put words to the nakedness I felt in her gaze, the shame of
inadequacy. Shivers racked my body.
  "What is it you really want, Devon? Devon? What is it you really
want?"
  For some reason, in her presence, my emotions felt raw, I could not
hold them back. Tears slid down my cheeks. "What I think you have," I
said.
  She rose from the bed and came to where I sat in the chair by the
window. She laid a hand on my head and pulled my head forward and
laid my face between her breasts. We remained in that position, my arms
wrapped around her waist, my tears cascading down her stomach, her

54

hand stroking the back of my neck. When my tears finally ceased and the shivering abated, she leaned close to my ear and whispered, "Now listen."

I stilled myself. I held my breath.

"And what do you hear?" she asked.

I could hear the flicker of a hundred candle flames. I could hear a moth going at the front window again. But loudest of all was a dull chilling roar.

"The wind blowing through my heart," I said.

She stroked my neck, she held me close. "I know, baby boy. Let it blow. Just let it blow."

Our lovemaking was different that night, it was more tender and giving. We did not seem to be working toward something with our touches and embrace but enjoying for its own sake each lingering kiss of skin upon skin, each inhalation of each other's scent, each subtly flavored taste upon the tongue.

It was an hour or so after midnight, at that time of morning when the cooling air begins to smell of mist and memory, when all sounds hush as if the sky has softly lowered itself as a blanket over the earth, as we lay side by side so still that I thought she was sleeping, she slipped her little hand against mine, fingers lacing between mine, and she asked, "What is the happiest you have ever been?"

Because before her question I had been aware of not a thought in my head, none of the usual clatter and clash, I answered, "Probably now."

"Another time," she said.

"This feels pretty good. Maybe the best ever."

Her hand lay against mine like a small crab that, on its arduous trip across the ocean floor, has paused to rest in half an empty shell. The shell wanted to close around the little crab and keep it there, hold it snug forever, but a broken shell lacks the ability to confine.

"Another time," she said.

I wanted to please her, so I searched my mind for a happy time. Childhood seemed the natural place to look but in every unraveling scene there were shadows and stains, arguments and curses, as if every photograph of memory kept in the scrapbook of my mind had been damaged in a fire, soot blackened or seared.

She must have sensed my struggle. "Don't strain, Devon. Just let it come."

I closed my eyes. A strange sensation ensued. My body seemed to sink further down into softness while my consciousness, some other part of self, rose up to the ceiling. What it saw when it looked down was a calm blue day maybe two years past. It was late afternoon and the sea was still. Jasper had shut off the engine and we were drifting with the current. He did that sometimes before taking us in, a slow drift for a while in the absence of chores. What he did in the wheelhouse on those occasions I hardly knew; enjoyed a cold beer maybe, an unhurried cigarette. Sometimes, it seemed, he was reluctant to go home. As for me, I lay across a tool chest on the foredeck, my back and shoulders aching from picking mostly debris but also a few fish from the net, then cleaning the fish and packing them in ice. With my head on hard metal I watched the slow scud of clouds above, felt the slow rise and fall below. Water lapped against the hull, a gull cried out. We had fish in the ice chest that day but not enough to account for the peace I felt. There was never enough fish for that. It was something about the movement, I think. The freshness of air, the lowering sun warm on my face, that lemony light.

What I felt that day, for a half hour maybe, felt something like a sigh between space and time, an interlude of emptiness where no space or time existed.

Was that happiness? I wondered, and felt Louisa Cecelia's hand move in mine.

"One day on the boat," I told her. "A kind of . . . nothing special time. We were drifting, that's all. But for a while I felt . . . ."

I searched for the words. Her fingertip rubbed a circle on my palm.

"I don't know," I said. "I just felt . . . all right. Like everything was . . . you know. Everything was just fine."

She asked for nothing more and for that I was grateful. I did not want to use words like harmony or serenity. I did not want to talk about grace. Still, I had to wonder: did she understand? I hardly understood myself.

Another hour passed, her hand in mine. When her breathing slowed and deepened, became a soothing rhythmic sibilance, I moved to slip out of bed. But this time her hand tightened around mine. So I eased close a while longer, our bodies touching along their lengths, her heel hooked over my shin. And in this position, fingers still interlaced, we slept.

A gust of wind awoke me, the rattle of a windowpane. When I looked to the window I saw that moonlight had been replaced by the gray of dawn. I had passed the night in her bed. Tiny drops of rain were pelting the window and running in streaks down the glass. I knew I could sleep no longer, so I slipped from her side and quietly dressed. Just as I reached the threshold and was about to leave the room, my shoes in hand, she said, "Thank you for the time you have given me, Devon."

I turned to her. She lay curled on her side now, face turned toward the window. And by that I knew that our time was done. With that knowledge, a terrible feeling of loss swept through me. My chest ached, my eyes stung. I looked about the room a last time, wanted to seize all the tiny details of her life that darkness had concealed from me, wanted each of those guttering candle flames to burn itself in my memory. I felt as if my home were being wrenched from me. I did not think I could bear it.

"Nothing is ever lost," she said, "unless you choose to lose it."

I might have argued that it was not my choice to leave her. But what good does argument do? I went into the next room, put on my shoes, and walked out to meet the rain.

I slept all through that day and night, awakening only once, just before midnight. I telephoned Jasper on his cell because I knew that he shuts it off at night and I did not want him to receive my message until morning. "Any chance you could run me over to the mainland on your way out to the Dwyers in the morning? I'm sorry to leave you like this, brother, but . . . . I'll meet you at the slip at six."

It is morning now and the air is chill and it carries the scent of a weather change. I am standing on the dock where *The Egg* should be moored but the slip is empty, nothing but water. I wonder if Jasper arrived early and has taken the boat to be fueled up. But he always fills the tanks the night before because the pumps don't open until seven, and it is still a few minutes to six. I stand on the edge of the dock and gaze out to sea, search the horizon for the silhouette of a boat.

I am confident that Jasper will be showing up soon. Soon I will hear the burbling growl of the old Johnson engine, and when he sees me from the wheelhouse he will greet me with a blast from the airhorn. Minutes later I will stand at the rail and watch Hogg Island growing small. A half hour later he will shake my hand and tell me to stay in touch and I will carry my bag onto another shore.

But as if to drive home the futility of planning, the faultiness of foresight, I hear a scuffling sound at my back, turn and see a smiling Jasper coming down the launch road to the dock. He carries a paper cup of The Sow's Ear's coffee in each hand.

I point to the empty slip. "Where's *The Egg*?"

First he hands me a cup of coffee, then he digs into his back pocket and comes up with one of those white plastic eggs that pantyhose are sold in. "Here you go," he says.

"What is this supposed to be?"

"Open it up."

Inside is a fat roll of bills. "No way," I tell him, and snap the egg together again. "I'm not taking your money."

"I sold *The Egg*, brudda. That's your share of the profits."

"Somebody bought it?"

He grins and sips his coffee. Then, "The Maritime Commission. They're so fucking eager to thin the fleet and put us draggers out of business. Believe it or not, we actually made a few bucks on the deal."

"All right," I say.

"Fucking right it's all right. It's fucking superlative."

The coffee is strong and black, the first sip of coffee I have had in weeks.

"I don't suppose you can tell me anything about . . . you know," he says.

"Not really."

"You have an idea where you're going?"

"Not really."

I fish into my pocket and bring out the truck key, then hand it to Jasper. "It's parked at The Sow's Ear. Do with it what you want."

"Sell it for scrap?"

"Sounds good to me."

We sip our coffee and smile at each other.

Then Jasper squints and leans closer. "What's the matter with your eyes?"

"What do you mean?"

"They used to be crossed."

"They aren't anymore?"

"You didn't notice?"

""I haven't looked in a mirror. Not since . . . a while back."

"They're not fucking crossed."

"I'll be damned," I say.

"You haven't been to a doctor?"

"I haven't been anywhere."

"I'll be damned," he says.

We grin at each other.

"So no *Egg*," I say. "I guess I'll just hang around and wait for the ferry. What day is this anyway?"

"It's Monday."

"So I only have forty-eight hours to wait."

"Naw, I made some calls this morning. Grody is going to take us over."

"Us?" I ask.

"Hey, I'm on vacation. What the fuck else do I have to do?"

"What time is he coming?"

"Six."

"Which for Grody means sometime after seven."

"Right. So let's just drink our coffee and enjoy this morning, what do you say?"

"It's good coffee."

"Fucking right," he says.

So we stand together at the end of the dock and we gaze upon the water. I have stood on this spot a thousand times and looked out across the water through the mist of morning, looked to the thin demarcation where sea and sky meet, but no morning has ever looked or felt like this one. We are all the same integers every morning, man and boat and dock and sea and sky, but every morning there is always a subtle difference to each of us. The sum of the parts is never the same. Life, I realize, is not a hard science. It is a constant bombardment of fluidity, a ceaseless pelting from all angles. Boats rot and take on water and sink and deteriorate. Slips stand empty. Bodies go down with the boats or float to the surface.

The waves roll in and cover the shore rocks and glide away again, roll and slide, touch and retreat. The wind rolls over the grass, smoothes it down, swirls around and pushes it up. My feet on a dock, air pushing me down, water buoying me up. It is all a continual dance, atoms and particles, breath against breath. I stand here on the splintered planking and I can feel the subtle movements, the ocean's rhythm, the planet's turn.

The waves roll in to slap the pilings and slosh against the dock. And what the water tells me is that the ocean's time is not man's time. The ocean's time is faster than the time of rocks, of mountain time and canyon time, but slower than the time that runs through forest and meadow and river and swamp. The trick for a man, the extreme difficulty if he wants to sense—for he can never understand—what is happening in those slower time zones beyond his own, is to synchronize his chronology with theirs. This can be accomplished only a moment or two at a time. In the silence, for example, between two heartbeats.

I am working on making those silences wider. There is so much to hear in the emptiness.

Wallace Stegner once said something to the effect that you cannot know who you are until you know where you are. I am here on Hogg Island and I am no longer here. I am with Louisa Cecelia and I will never be with her again. I am in and of Devon Hawkins, soon to board the dragger *Joanna*, soon to be in transit to unknown places where the strange will be familiar and the familiar will be strange. Finding my way to the slip this morning was the hard part. All the rest should be easy.

"So you and Queenie," Jasper says. "You two, you know, do anything interesting together? Anything you can talk about?"

"I read her some stories. Two stories and a poem."

"Oh yeah?"

"Yep."

"I'll bet you fucking bored her to death, didn't you?"

The water laps at the pilings, it gurgles and laughs.